CW01184814

Wo

Wonders

Wanderings

a collection of poems

by

Brenda Hooson

Published by the author.

Printed by Kindle Direct Publishing.

© Brenda Hooson, 2021

FROM THE AUTHOR

Moving to Little Baddow from Southend-on-Sea in 1968, on marriage to John, my little black book already had quite a collection of poems in it. After the 2nd World War, entertainment was down to oneself, but life as an only child was never lonely. My parents always encouraged me to make friends, and to develop my curiosity in the natural world, by naming birds, learning their songs, and naming plants and flowers, both garden and wild.

The village of Little Baddow, our destined place, chosen because it was a green oasis on the map, with the advantage of a not too distant train to the City, has always been a joy and privilege to reside in.

Quite soon I had no need of a train, as we began our family. Walking with children, dogs, sometimes cats, gave me opportunities to absorb the beauty at our fingertips.

In writing poems, I have used my love of words, the fun of rhythm, rhyme, to illustrate memories gathered from everyday experiences and UK holidays. Poetry is all about sound, and should be read aloud – my two daughters and granddaughter are well-versed in them! Many *have* been used in Chapel services and talks to various groups locally. Putting them in print, for all to share, has been one of the happier consequences of the Covid pandemic.

Brenda Hooson
May 2021

THE POEMS

Reflections

When flowers abound in the meadow;
When cow parsley stands shoulder high;
When butterflies bask in the sunshine,
And larks throw their songs from the sky
It's then I reflect on my fortune
To live in this wonderful place.

Remember that time in the winter?
The fields then were brown, save the frost
Which sparkled on top of each furrow,
And silvered each leaf autumn lost.
The cow parsley stood by, quite barren,
Its hidden seed waiting for spring;
While frosted the starry heads shimmered:
New meaning to each one did bring.

Remember the fresh greens of springtime;
Bright mustard seed high on the hill;
The scent and the carpet of bluebells;
White stitchwort the hedgerow did frill:
The trees wore their bonnets of blossom;
While gardens were filled with great charm,
As daffodils danced in the sunshine,
And azaleas burst into bloom.

Now autumn's fairness is with us,
And replacing the once golden corn
Are bare fields, all ploughed, and now planted.
A new crop already is sown.
Whilst here in my own little garden,
Leaves burnish and berries glow red;
Joyous sparrows a-throng in the tree tops,
And lapwings cry out overhead.

THE WAGTAILS

Hid by a curtain
A curtain of green
The waters leap
With frightening speed
And deafening roar
To chasms deep.
Nature seems hushed by
The awe of it all
Save the yellow bird
Who wags his tail as
He gobbles up the
Flies the water stirred.

By an old bridge where
Stones need to be passed
The river glides,
Slowing to capture
The radiant colours
Of flowers nearby.
On tiptoe just creep
Right up to the bridge
And take a peep through.
There, dabbling, darting
And bobbing about,
Are wagtails here too.

(Grey Wagtails,
North Wales.)

Summer Meadow

Only grasses sway in the breeze
But wait and watch:
Wait 'till the sun throws off the sleaze
Of a tardy dawn;
Warms with care every folded wing
Of the herby roost.
Then it's alive with fluttery things
As butterflies wake
And hov'ring moths – like Silver Ys
Seek a nectar sip.
Those Blues and Coppers still to rise,
A Tortoiseshell basks
Beside a Small (and sleepy) Heath
Its wings tight closed.
But chestnut sheen with orange "teeth"
Brown Argus boasts.
Atop the Hardheads perched enticingly –
The moment brief.
In flight they look surprisingly
Like scraps of foil:
Catching light as they seem to dance; dance
For the 'meadow band'.

Note: 'meadow band' means grasshoppers!

October 1996

THE CHARM

An old, old house is Poleighs, weatherworn;
Moulded through centuries by rain and storm
Sunshine and shower;
Undaunted it smiles, bedecked with posies,
And hugs to itself the scented roses,
And tangled bower
Of honeysuckle's fragrance by the door.
Their feet no doubt, beneath the firewarmed floor
When frosts abide.
But perfumed evenings are a fine reward
For all the protection the house affords.
While step inside
And spirits both of past and present, rise
In friendly greeting.

How lovely to sit by the fireside glow:
To peep through the window at glistening snow
All frosty and white.
Or watch with amusement tit acrobats
Hanging and jostling for beakfuls of fat
Suspended outside.
Maybe a mouse from the woodpile will creep,
Gathering (cheekily) crumbs from the heap
Of bread for the birds.
Red robin will come – thrush and blackbird too,
When they have nestlings and much to do,
And make themselves heard.
A quick snack is all they need. Then away –
Back to the youngsters.

Somehow the house and the garden seem one:
A mingling of smells; a cake just begun;
Rich bubbling jam;
The perfume of lilies adrift on the air;
Ripening tomatoes for all to share;
The fruity tang
Of sunkissed apples on a bending bough:
The sweetness of earth, and flowers rain-dowsed;
The new-mown grass.

A bowl of blossom with colours gay,
Placed in the window to brighten the day
Of all who pass,
Or venture inside for a friendly chat
Or a cup of tea.

Then today while I was a visitor there,
Other visitors came, quite unaware
Of voices or knitting.
They came singing gently, bell-like and sweet
And each settled quickly for something to eat,
Red heads a-bobbing.
Enframed in the window, wings trimmed with sun's braid,
Plucking at seedheads by Michaelmas made,
Those goldfinches perched.
Intent on feeding (such delicious fare)
Unheeded were the exhuberant stares
With which we watched
This little charm. Surely this is the charm
Of the old, old house.

September

Have you seen the summer fading?
Have you smelled the misty morn?
A myriad rainbow dewdrops
Lie a-sparkling on the lawn.
In the garden and the hedgerow
Berries hang, a glossy red,
While somewhere in the branches
Robin sings as leaves are shed,
Lazy notes that tell of autumn
With the fall that is to come,
Tinted leaves and golden chestnuts
Polished, glowing in the sun.

Have you watched the harvest moonrise?
Have you heard the owls call?
Eerie notes, at once delighting in
So huge an orange ball.
Later, silver overflowing
From the heaven to earth below,
Touched so gently by the moonbeams
All the countryside's aglow.
Beneath this radiance gleaming
Fields of stubble now
Await tomorrow's crying seagulls
And the furrows of the plough.

(1972)

FAIRY DANCING

What of these miracles unwinged
That ride on Summer's dying breath:
That drift with purpose far a-field
Then slowly sink to dew-soaked earth?
These spores of microscopic dust
Within their cells possess, diverse
Shapes and sizes; such subtle shades;
And those that wait beneath the wood
For Autumn and her morning raids
To shower down the burnished leaves,
Know just the one for promenades
Beneath the waving trees.

With sprightly speed they set to work;
And there before my eyes next day
Are funnel cups, and shining caps
Of bronze and russet, fawn and grey.
Some speckled red, or freckled white,
Plum, and gold in clusters gay.
As if by magic, each one knows
The kind of leaf its resting by:
And so each different fungi grows.
But I, who only come to watch,
See countless fairy dancing shows
With parasols to match.

EARLY WARNING

Who was it that chided the North Wind?
Did Autumn leave open the Gate?
He certainly came uninvited
And His fury is not yet spent.
With wildness He tears at the washing;
Strips leaves in His bitter-cold rage;
Howls round the house like a demon,
His foothold the old chimney vent.

There He whines like a child frustrated
For no-one will let Him come in.
He even tries lifting the roof tiles,
And rattles both windows and doors.
Defeated He roars even louder;
In anger throws over the bin;
Still no-one within bids Him enter,
So He sneaks; icy drafts cross the floor.

Tomorrow we'll count the destruction
Derived from this savage pursuit.
He's gone, but it's only a respite;
A sulky retreat, leaving frost
To blacken with harshness the herbage,
And a warning portrayed in "old truth".
As in the poem "The North Wind doth blow",
Then we shall have snow – to our cost!

Blessings from Heaven

Raindrops round and bright
Catching beams of light.
Flashing and splashing,
Endlessly dashing
Tinkling, pattering:
This cool, spattering,
Life-giving shower
Sparkles on flowers;
And if, by some chance
The sun sports a glance,
Then I will see, too,
A wonderful hue:
The world so embraced
By an archway in space.

Snowflakes fat and white,
Such a pretty sight,
Spinning and swirling,
Dizzyly twirling;
Suddenly, floating
Without a motive
It seems: suspended.
Then they look splendid.
Now I can catch them;
Examine them, gems
That they are. From where
Did such beauty dare
To come, to grace so
Small a flake of snow?

A Special Day

A final snowflake fluttered, twirled
To an unknown rest
As in the east, a sleepy sun
Meekly did its best
To chase away the cold, dark night
With a rosy glow;
And chase afar the heavy clouds
So laden with snow.

No-one had seen their coming, deep
    In the hush of night.
No-one had heard the sighing breeze
    So gentle and light
That wafted the snowflakes down to
Earth – their newfound home –
Hugging close the boughs of the trees;
    Or warming the loam.

A robin in the hollybush
    Saw the blushing sky;
The deep pure snow, lacy trees and
    Thought that he would fly
To the fir tree by the mereside
    There alone to watch
The sun tint all that snowy scene
    Palest pink to match.

Not a ripple stirred the water.
All was calm and still,
'Til the robin in the fir tree
    Lifted high his bill
And sang his blessing to the morn,
    Notes so clear and sweet
That ev'n the awak'ning thrush
    Could not its challenge meet.

It was at this very moment
    Many birds a-sing
The the bells of the Parish Church
    Joyously did ring.
Peel after peel rang over the
    Magical white lay
News that everyone should know – that
    This was Christmas Day.

Ellesmere, Shropshire

Winter Images

All snowmen complete
With hat and scarf, red rosy nose,
Stare out from coaly eyes:
Snowballers retreat
With fingers blue, ten frozen toes,
To warm beside the fire;
And delighted shrieks
From some young toboggonists' fun
Fade long before the thaw.

Thick mantle of snow
Within which lies a multitude
Of differing symmetry:
In numbers unknown
But with delicate aptitude
Flakes pattern mundanity;
Soften the landscape:
Until we see only beautiful
Sparkling prisms of light.

Indolent sunbeams
Yet imbuing the woodside
From that feeble glow
With peaches and cream,
While long shadows of its trees slide
Slowly to evening.
One single star gleams,
Mocking such warmth the West implies,
For here creeps frozen night.

By moonbeams bestirred
And tall hopes of desperate mice
An owl hoots. His cry
Alone Jack Frost disturbs
Who breathes, creates and fashions ice;
Scatters gems; silvers buds;
Gives twiglets furs:
While clouds like angels in full flight
Adorn the heavens.

Come morning's pearl light
When eager birds, crisp skiddy roads
Combine to make us care:
Recall then how bright
Each crystallized vapour-drop glows
When carressed by the sun;
And look with fresh sight,
For heavens abandoned clouds
Commend the world anew.

The Sky

The warmth of sunshine brings a smile
 A gladness to the heart.
As does the calmness of the sea
 Beneath a rainbow's arch

But clear blue sky gives more than this –
 A glimpse worth more than gold
Its colour, depth, infinity
 Inspire a hungry soul.

JUST NEIGHBOURS

Two swallows returned to their nest, Bonny's stable
    Weary with winging the world,
But saw at a glance that they were no longer able
    To raise any young there themselves.
Some wrens had moved in and by clever conversion
The mud cup, when cleared of its dross,
And entrance made tiny by fitting insertions.
    Was rendered entirely in moss.
Undaunted those swallows flew fresh mud to the site
    And beginning bare inches away
Built a new home and settled without any fight
    In this, the good-neighbourly way!

Prospection

Come. February, come!
My heart delights to hear
The Mistle chant his haunting song,
For surely spring is near.

Come, February, come,
Break through the steely skies,
For warmth and sun and gentleness
My spirit, craving, cries.

Come, February, come:
With birds in chorus blend.
Announce that winter slowly dies;
That spring a soft hand lends.

Go, February, go.
Dally not one day
Amid the drooping heralds where
Shy snowdrops sweetly sway.

Somewhere

There in the marsh untrod by men,
A quite distinguished bird does live.
Stalking about with careful tread
His prey he fools so easily.
For nature clothed him mindfully
And gave him feathers regal gold
But tinged them brown; so like the reeds
Themselves he is. Alarmed he'll hold
Himself erect, and silently
Direct his beak so pointedly
Towards the sky, that merged is he
In the swaying grass, and no-one,
Friend or foe, can that bittern see,
But when his booming voice rings out,
Everyone knows without a doubt.

Which way to Heaven?

I wish you could see the Tulip trees:
A host of angels singing.
Dazzling our eyes with a brilliance
Of a pastel-petalled crowd;
Clouds of prayer just winging
Their way to heaven.

I'd love you to hear the chiff-chaff
Acclaim from orchard bough
That Spring, with all its multitude
Of blossoms bright and beautiful,
Has returned to England now,
And earth *is* heaven.

BIRTHDAYS

March comes with icy finger
And blanket of snow
While deep in earth still sleepy
Plants flourish and grow.
Each at its heart a flower
In colour so bright
Save the first few, the snowdrops
So pure and so white.
March goes – leaving glories
Of blossoms to come;
A promise of green leaves
And hot summer sun.

YOUNG MARTIN

Exhausted – he showed no fear of capture.
Rather, a wide-eyed puzzlement
At human surroundings, voices, stature,
Dark eyes regarding his immediate world
From his perch on the back of my hand.
With just an inborn instinctive wish to fly;
To spread his wings and feel the wind
Lift him as it did at dawn, from nest to sky.

Lovingly, we placed him overnight to rest,
Hoping he would warmly sleep in
His tiny box and unfamiliar nest.
So it was when morning came, blustery, bright,
We found him eager to be off,
And carrying him to where the wind was strong
Threw him high, high into the breeze.
A few unsteady beats, and then he was gone.

FREEDOM

Consider a Jay's feather:
Symbol of earth and heaven.
Staunch reminder of days past;
Certain hope of future's joy.
A little child holds fast
To this, sees with deeper vision,
As Jacob saw the ladder
Massed with iridescent wings
In the bluest, bluest sky.
What of me? I see the bird
Flash wings; (Lapis lazuli –
Gems of Solomon's Temple!)
Fly with purpose through a wood,
While man who builds the Temple,
Holy, worthy place for God,
Creates chaos in His world;
Confuses principles of
Love with those of ownership;
Walks hand in hand with greed;
Thirsts for wisdom, knowledge, but
Forgets so simple logic.
But He, designing detail
With such a wondrous magic
Flies free, and waits with patience
To clothe us ALL with feathers!

THE VISITORS

Oh gypsies of the sky
    Where now do you roam?
Have you left your earthly nest
    For heaven your home?

Warm summer air
Hunting ground of the swifts
How they love it!
Their screams of wild delight
Fill me with joy.
Oft times I watch and wish
That I could fly
With them to thrilling height,
There to glide and
Twist with careless ease; or
Join their game of
Catch about the houses.
Such speed and grace
Precision which is theirs
And theirs alone,
My wonder arouses,
My envy, too.

What beauty they must see
Travelling wide:
Tackling the blue like yachts
Upon the tide;
Or tirelessly winging
To hotter lands.
I search the sky for spots,
But see not one:
No sign of distant wings.
At sundown though
Ghostly cries float down …
From some other
World … reminders of
The pleasant days
Those gypsies came to town!

Recompense

Why *hate* a rainy day?

The starlings probe the lawn for grubs;
For them an easy hour;
The roses scent each moisture drop;
And all the elder flowers
Look just like granny's lacy mats
A-bobbing in the breeze.

Why hate a rainy day?

Beside the stream a blackcap sings
With joyous bubbling glee;
A songthrush on the rooftop high;
A blackbird in the tree.
If they are all so thankful –
Then why should I not be?

Each puddle's grey with scudding cloud;
I tread and wellies squelch;
While leaves full-blown send showers down –
Cool droplets on my neck.
The washing has to hang indoors,
And dog-art has its day
As muddy paw-prints liven up
The kitchen in some way!

Though everywhere's so very wet
And flowers drink their fill,
The rain it comes relentless, on:
The wind when will it still?
Then suddenly the sun is out;
Blushed misty-pink the hill;
Each skyward leaf and petal gay
So prettily bejewelled –

Why *hate* a rainy day?

Through the Window

The choice of pantry window sill
Drew busy wings and feet and bill,
A nest to fashion in a trice
From grasses, moss, and all things nice –
For us to see.

For days the blackbird brooded there
Unblinkingly – content to stare
At human curiosity.
We had no animosity –
Just came to see.

At last from eggs of greenish-blue
Floundered fleshy fledglings new;
Three tiny wobbly jelly beans
Who needed constant wormy feeds
They could not see.

Each day they gaped a thousand times,
And swallowed ants, and moths and flies –
Just anything their parents brought
Until one day a change was wrought
For they could see.

From dawn to dusk the babes were fed
While daily changes came and went.
From skin to fluff and thence to feather,
Stretched their wings, or slept together.
What fun to see!

The morning came when wings were strong,
And took the birds where they belong
To hide among the apple leaves,
The empty nest – we're *very* pleased.
For all to see.

Meadow Saxifrage

Within the wrinkled bulbil
All seems asleep.
Presupposed! Mysteriously
Life vigil keeps:
Undeterred by Winter's bite
Roots downward creep,
Leaves between Jack's frosted grass
Soft-furry peep.

So dreams this little bulbil
Of heights unseen.
A pink-nosed bud on hairy stem
Swells dandy green,
Until unclasped from Nectar's pot
Pure petals gleam.
The pearly gates of heaven
For Maytime's Queen.

THE RIPENING

God walked in the garden – it was beautiful there:
July had been with her braided hair.
Gold skirts aswish as breeze blown wheat,
She'd passed with grace
And harebelled feet through the churchyard gates.
God walked in the garden … His eye not cast
On delicate harebells in the grass
But on apples.

The Bright Side

Puddle dirty, infinitely murky,
  What joys do you hold?
The laughter of children, a drink for the bold.

Puddle dirty, infinitely murky,
  A use I can tell.
As bathplace for birdlife you perform very well.

Puddle dirty, infinitely murky,
  What mysteries you bear,
When frozen a crystalized leaf will appear.

Puddle dirty, infinitely murky,
  What beauty in sight.
White sailings by day seek the gold ship of night.

A Dog's Life

Our Percy you'd say was a Shropshire lad
Born Suskim Cavalier on a farm there.
Percy the Pup was both naughty and bad,
Percy was bad but we loved him.

We named him Persimmon – his Sunday name –
A racehorse, a train, a dark plum-like fruit.
Taking our shoes off his favourite game,
Percy was fun and we loved him.

He ran with great speed whenever he could,
I'd wait at the Holybred footpath post
While he'd swiftly fast-circuit the wood.
P the P clever – we loved him.

At home any teatowel was dragged round the floor;
Post became paper reduced to fine shreds.
If anyone knocked – well he'd open the door!
P oh so boisterous – we loved him.

His lifetime collection of other dogs' toys
Took over his toybox or littered the floor.
Add "squashy bottles" – his recycling ploy.
Percy was great – and we loved him.

Percy liked curry especially rice,
Toastcrusts at lunchtime – marmalade please.
His food Eukanuba (with catfood!) was nice.
Percy so gentle we loved him.

Strange dogs were a problem, he liked to be boss,
Some he would tip up to prove who was who.
Others, like Frankie, he'd wind up of course.
Mischievous P – but we loved him.

A long window table he found just ideal
For watching, waiting for sounds of our car.
At night-time hearth-napping quite lost its appeal,
The sofa for Percy, we loved him.

Persimmon lived to a good 'Flattie' age.
Like Harriet cat, he's gone just beyond
So now we must turn another new page,
P the free spirit. We loved him.

DIAMOND

A diamond's but a lump of rock –
The bowels of earth embellished;
Received as lover's token true
This jewel is highly cherished.
Bright stars create a diamond sky;
Distilled at dawn is diamond dew:
While those who've wed for sixty years
Will celebrate in diamond too.
But none of these can yet surpass
The sparkle of two loving hearts.

(for Roy and Elizabeth Warsop)

THE BAY

Budle – where sky strokes the sea
With ever-changing hues of blues and green.
Budle – where sands of silver lie
As velvet cushions to the probing tide.
Budle – where strong retreating waves
Leave intriguing patterns – dinosaur tails?
Budle and pools the Godwits know;
Mud blotted out by flakes of seagull snow
Budle – watch the dying rays
Guild the straight and narrow: God's golden way.
Budle – see the lighthouse beam.
Complete computer vigilance: we may dream.
Budle – hear the ocean thrum,
Constant in pitch blackness: our day is done.
Budle – still the Cuddies cry.
Do they search for Cuthbert on his "windswept Isle"?
Budle – sense the sounds so pagan –
Homeless spirits roaming since St Aidan?
Budle twixt two castles set.
It wasn't always peaceful, let us not forget.
Budle – where Sea-pie, Curlew call
To rouse the hare and welcome in the dawn.
Budle – its magic is still there ..
Build a castle in the sand – come who dare!

THE GIFT

Take a glass of water,
Clear, motionless, weak;
Boil it and it disappears,
Vapour on transparent wings.
Take a cloud,
Shaped by the invisible;
Cooled and transformed into
Intricate crystals, no two alike.
Take a raindrop,
Tiny, insignificant,
Yet without its prism
The rainbow would never be seen.
Take a pool,
Seemingly lifeless;
A trickle even, trapped:
Frozen its strength can split rock,
Take a spring
Welling into gurgles,
Escaping, gathering momentum:
A river instinctively flowing,
Gushing, cascading;
A waterfall:
And there you have energy
Sufficient to warm a million homes.
Take the sea.
Ah! The invincible sea,
Without which neither I nor the world
Could ever have been.
Take a glass of water!

The Bunch

A gift without sentiment: merely "because".
Sweet Peas they were – purple and mauve.
In form reminiscent of heavenly things
Arched petals as silky smooth wings.
Exquisitely scented each perfumed my room
Expelling dull skies and deep gloom.
The vase stands now empty its flowers long gone,
Ghost fragrance alone lingers on.

Colour Fast

Green shadows in the water
Of the cockle boats in file:
Green marshes by the river:
Green hedges by the style:

Green is the meadow,
But mottled with gold;
Green is the background
For colours untold:

Patches of scarlet,
Splashes of white
Sprinkling of purple
Pretty and bright;
Carpets of lemon,
Here and there blue
Pale as the sky on
Morns full of dew.

Honey and beige;
Orange – a trace;
Lilac and pink –
Delicate lace.
Next a rich peach
Fading to rose:
Yellow so deep;
Violet, mauve.

Fields full of mustard
Awaiting the bee;
Under the hedges
A blue like the sea:
Scarcer and rarer
So showing its worth
Royal blue stretches
Proud of its birth.
Autumn comes soon –
It's amazing I feel
That so many colours
In so short a summer
Spring out of the ground
… Out of the ground
Out of the … ground.

This is now a historic poem (written on the train in August 1966 from Southend East to Fenchurch Street) as the modern trains no longer make this sound!

Rosedale

Today we walked where a railway once ran,
Enterprisingly built by industrious man.
As mile after mile the trackbed we trod,
We tried to imagine the buildings that stood
And instead of the silence substitute sound
Of creaking wagons – vibrating ground;
The sound of voices of men at work;
Children playing – a chicken's squawk:
For moving the iron ore load by load
From the mountainside to the nearest road
Was a task that brought whole families here,
High up in the dale, to live year by year.

It's difficult now to picture them there
With little but rubble to show us just where
The cottages stood. The manager's house –
The workshops are gone. Magnificent grouse
Patrol there instead; strutt lordly about
Wherever they please, their calls seeming loud
In the quiet. We saw the great open shaft:
A blacksmith worked near at his craft
Of shoeing, and sharpening, forging the hammers.
Now just the wheatear insects do gather,
While high on the kiln kestrels hungrily cry
Like ghosts of the railway reluctant to die.

Partiality

Those days are the best
When the valley is shrouded in mist;
Trees partially veiled: future glimpsed
Like Chinese art,
And pylons the ladders to heaven.
Those days are the best
When I wake with a smile,
Illogical though it seems
For there's little to smile about.
But yet my heart sings with the birds:
Those days are the best.

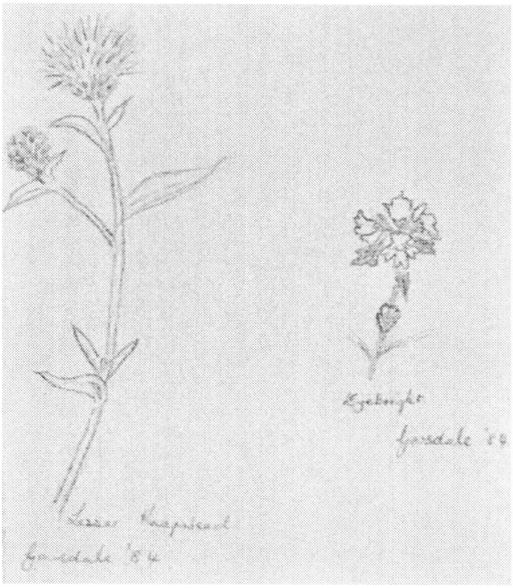

The Tenth Month

October showers russet shapes
Fast twirling ochre keys
Of sycamore and ash.
She welcomes with wide open arms,
Fieldfare, redwing, fresh
From Northern frosting shores.
With golden morns and blushy skies
She tints the guelder rose;
Flames arching bramble nooks;
And leans toward those icy hours
Of ruddy cheeks and nose:
Dark nights of Winter's grip.

Transcending

Love wrought my eyes that I might see
    Beyond the far horizon:
Love gave me ears which clearly hear
    The soundlessness of God.
Love formed my body's intricacy
    And taught my soul to sing,
But best of all the Spirit's gifts,
    Love lends my heart its wings.

SEPARATION

Far beyond reed and brackish marsh,
Scrip-scrapy sounds of noisy gulls,
            The sea.
In greyish turbulence it thrashed
And as it crashed upon the shore,
            Drew me
Like someone hypnotized, to stare,
At countless crested wavelets touched
            With blue,
In wonder that this writhing mass
Kept secrets still, and somehow led –
            To dew.

Brief Sighting

At the edge of the tide the waders search,
Probing the mud for the luscious food.
Running this way – dashing that –
Then suddenly, with a change of mood
They each fly up with one accord
A woosh of wings and a piping cry.
Now all that's left, is the mud, the sea,
And a clear expanse of the endless sky.

Party Mice

It's quiet today in Holybred Wood,
Not a breath of wind stirs.
The badgers are sleeping deep down in
their setts
But high in the firs
A party of titmice are creeping about,
Their faces so nice;
Their long tails a-peeping between
the fircones
Like sugar-pink mice.

Counterpart

See – the tiniest sliver of moon so fine,
Curved as a tangerine segment;
Light as a fingertip tracing a smile:
Etched on azure heavens, a silver shimmery line
Deepening as night-moth's velvet
Stretches, flies, spreads honey-suckle wings.
Thoughts of a parting linger, sharpening my mind
Til stars somersault, become daisies
Hugging tight the rosy-tipped dawn;
And the heart that flips like stars into flowers
is mine.

The Clouded Yellow Year

It's gone – they've gone!

The old year, transient as fine wings
Unable to survive the cold, dies,
Leaving only a faintest recollection
Of those exquisite moments
When angels touched our countryside, flashed
Wings of gold across the Lucerne fields;
For they, their constant searching satisfied,
Each sleep the sleep of death.

31.12.92

Daybreak

Sweet robin – no better timed than this;
Blackbird calls and thrush his carol keeps
To welcome in the first light from the East:
But at your voice see darkness hasten
Before radiance streams full-blown and
Claims possession of another day.
Wren sings incessantly from dawn;
Greenfinch trills monotonously on;
A frog croaks, showering on the lawn;
They urge me add my silent thanks
For hours of love, and life ahead.

Failte do Ard nam Murchan (Welcome to Ardnamurchan)

Beyond the farm at Ockle
Dreams heather's copious haze,
A weave to cloak September's bays
Of tipsy basalt flows and pools,
Where surreptitious winkles glide;
Late limpets whirl: before the tide
Churns frothy, clinging foam to pipe
The fingers of the rocks.

Along the Point at Ockle
Preened gulls a cloud of wings:
More noble eider ride and sing,
In fearsome swirling eddies dive,
Spray-dowsed one resting shag looks on
As gannets soar: with muscles strong
Exploit the thermals high to plunge
On unsuspecting fish.

Within the Bay at Ockle,
Where ghosts of fishers past
Quietly bestir Parnassus Grass,
Are sable bogs with Butterwort;
Sphagnum rich in Sundew flowers:
How easy then to idle hours;
Search crystal crevices and peer,
Such magic lingers there.

Return then to Tigh Dochie:
It eyes the resting sun,
And so remote that wildlife come,
Ignore the inmates watchful air.
Soft peachy sea: there islands rise
To heights of apricot; while cries
From buzzards … hunting … gliding
Conclude a perfect day.

The Honour

While we board our massive jumbos,
    Our need to seek the sun:
A moth that's born of sultry air,
    Bright blossoms abundant,
Recalling more delicate scent
    Of an English garden,
Incredibly negotiates
    Europe in search of one!

(The Hummingbird Hawkmoth)

Loch Katrine

Beside stately firs so gracefully green
The fiery laden rowans lean,
With every vibrant fruited twig
Cascading down the mountainside,
Towards the place where heather roams;
Creates a hue all of its own:
While glistening hips, like rubies shine;
And wind-tossed bracken fronds entwine
Scabious – blue as a summer's sky,
But where just now, great clouds do fly,
Pursued relentlessly by wind,
Some subtly shaded, some like sins
Until with hilltops they collide,
And droplets for sweet earth provide.

We two, who cruise across the loch
This scene in fascination watch:
A persistent sun who ever dares
To taunt and flaunt without a care.
Reluctantly the clouds give way
And let the sunbeams dance and play
On the meadows green. See again!
Another shaft shines through the rain.
The rain that feels like the blown spume
While the Captain plays a Scottish tune.
We glance around in sun's bright glow,
And there above the hill – a 'bow'.
The colours of the spectrum span.
Such simple things – such joy to man!

THE SEVENTH DAY

Who may go up the mountain of the Lord?
And who may stand in his holy place?
Psalm 24

Ben Hiant Holy Mountain
Who was it named you so?
Maybe St. Columba for
Legend says that long ago
He passed though Ardnamurchan,
Baptised at Ardslignish.

So quiet, only midges moved,
Disturbed from their reverie
By our heavy-booted feet.
There among pale twirling "Heaths"
We glimpsed rare orchid revels
Plum-rich in velvet sheathes,
And pondered as we clambered,
Climbed up from the ridge, the day
Men paid no heed to plants, but
Ran in pursuit all in vain,
Whose hearts were full of murder
For Muchdragon was slain.

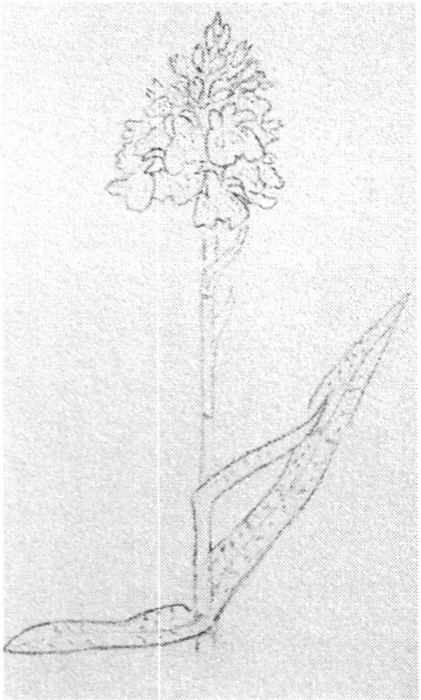

Ben Hiant – Holy Mountain,
Such bloodshed at your door.
Down through all the ages men
Fought their futile, feudal war:
Huge Norsemen and tough Vikings,
Clans, and Lords of the Isles.

Deafening silence! None could guess
The past. Scenically the same
Brave tapestry of hills and lochs.
Soft blue-green showed May's terrain
Melting into mill-pond seas,
A-sheen as best porcelain
Polished by some caring hand:
Gleaming, brushed by partial light
Of pastel clouds, whose pattern,
Heather-toned in lazy flight
Mirrored days that lie ahead
All robed in mauve delight.

Ben Hiant – Holy Mountain
Your peace forever keep
For those who reach the summit,
Though the way be rough and steep:
And standing see as we saw:
God shares this holy place.

Note: Muchdragon MacRi Lochlunn – Norwegian chief, tyrannical, licentious ruler killed in 1266 by Evun Cleireach – Evun the Clerk who lived at the foot of Ben Hiant.
Evun flung his battleaxe into the skull of the Norseman, fled to the summit pursued by Muchdragon's followers and made his escape because the men grabbed at his cloak and the material gave way. So while they fell backwards down the hill, Evun made his way to the shore where his wife and family waited in a boat.

THE LINK

Oli was born on the 'Water
One summer, offspring of Albert and Flo.
Shipcats aboard the boat Florence –
Taylor & Taylor were Skipper and Mate.

Oli had brothers and sisters
But was always intent on escape,
Swinging with greatest abandon.
Conquering easily new barricades.

Oliver, true to his namesake
In those early days did ask for more,
And after he came home to Baddow
Was frequently first at the door.

It was Harriet though who was
Vocal, commanding the food to be there
While Oli did most of the eating
From the saucer they both liked to share.

Together they terrified wildlife;
Were definitely in charge of our dogs,
Until that is we got Percy …
Then Oli, undaunted, *attempted* the job!

With loud purr endearingly constant
He'd play 'fierce' during making the beds.
Perhaps though this funniest habit –
A passion for breakfast's boiled eggs!

Oliver (1990 – 2001)

THE WIND OF CHANGE

Where once white blossom hung,
    The bough bends low
    With row on row
Of appetizing apples.

Where sprouted crisp green corn,
    The field is white
    (Oh! Such a sight.)
And each ear fat and ready.

Where once the earth was tilled,
    The farmer now
    Discards the plough
To gather in his harvest.

Where water showed the trees
    In spring-time scene
    All leaves were green.
Russet now is blended.

Where birds built nests and sang,
    Great numbers wait
    Until the date
Is right for their migration.

The Hurricane

Some monster this, who in one night
Destroyed, in numbered millions,
Trees that only hours before
Served nature's realm, gave us delight.

* * * *

Darkness, fear, no light at finger's touch;
Matches, candles, at least we'd got:
No telephone with cheery voice;
But still we coped, we had no choice:
And when at last the storm had gone
We learnt with shock the damage done.

Our roads as if huge bombs had struck;
Each wood a jumbled battleground.
Some trees who'd seen a hundred years
Of season's order come to pass
Would never know another day.
In sympathy we shared our tears
Stunned that for most this was the end –
How could we push them up again?
Their own kind knew the pain they bore
As wounded soldiers helpless lay,
This was no natural death for them
With limbs and living roots so torn.

Wind born from force of earth itself
With fiery eye and salty breath
Howled loud and drowned all Terror's screams.
Impossible to know just why
The ablest fell, the weakest stood;
Or understand the strength unseen
That snapped resistance clean in half:
A broken toy the finest oak.
But counting them as life for life
Our human minds may merely muse,
While sad our remedy's the saw,
We thank God for their sacrifice.

(16.10.87)

Parallel

Eager flame of life, leaps up,
    reaches out; touches briefly:
Dampened smoulders: unbidden
    one glowing ember flashes,
Longs for rekindling, waiting,
    Waning: numbed by the ultimate
A fate of white ashes.

Suppose within that cooling
    soporific dust, a pattern,
Steeped in luminosity
    merely slumbers … waiting.
Replaced on planet's earthy crust
    a miracle transpires, flowers:
Fire of God's creating.

(Lent, 1988)

Woodland Remnant

Heartbroken trees,
Their bulks lie prostrate on dark peat.
Yet valiantly innumerous twigs
A vigil with the Season keep,
As hour by hour, and drip by drip,
Instinctive as a river knows
Which route will doubtless reach the sea
The rising sap now streamlike flows:
All sleepiness in bud dispels,
Unfurls, renews a host of green
Inherent shapes, and culminates
In giant rollers, seas of leaves.

Amazingly,
Amid those tangled ripped-off roots,
Quite unperturbed sweet bluebells grow;
Push skyward, spears and flowing shoots,
Each muffled bell in readiness:
Carillons for the peal of Spring.
A yaffle calls, echoes intent
To drill a home in which to bring
Some fledglings up despite the loss.
His laughter joins those mist-blue bells
Defying fate. Spring's music floats
And ever, fresh with new life, swells.

Speciality

How calm the bare but spangled wood
On this December morn.
No breeze dispels the mistiness
While merest hints of wistfulness
Conveyed by leaves forlorn
Are banished as the "shoe shine boys"
Left all a waxy tan.

And there among the beaded twigs
Some goldcrests, never shy,
Show not a whit of bashfulness;
Flick tails and wings in playfulness;
Cock heads: they wear with pride
A tiny flash of gold, and yet
The finest Advent Crowns.

Moonshine

Under the Hollies a stage of leaves dry,
Who lingers may glimpse
when the night-wanderer's high,
A gleaming white spotlight
Full in the place
Where a moon-fairy dances
with elegant grace.

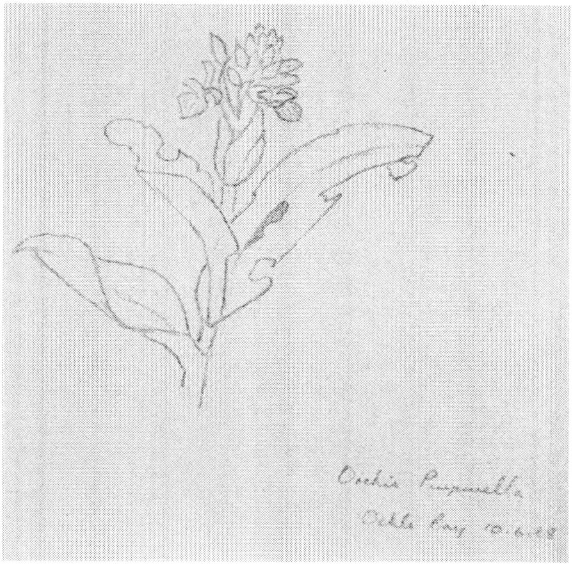

500 Years Ago

It seems that way sometimes
And then I look up and know
It was only days, minutes ago;
That time in itself is unimportant;
That time does not heal, only God
With His amazing knowledge of our souls
Seeks to do the impossible.

The heron, motionless
By the pool, waiting, watching,
Was there a thousand lifetimes back.

We must be as that pool,
Becalmed and reflective;
Not fretting when wind ripples come;
Nor rejecting; nor scaring things off.
Rather absorbing that which is true
As water the image of tree and bird,
Changing but indestructible.

The heron, "purple'-winged,
Flew off, but she'll return,
As she did five hundred years ago!

Quiet Day at The Barn, Newhall
December 1993
Theme: Time

Morning Watch

With feathers white as sparkling spume,
A keen dark eye and nimble legs
The sanderling came, and watching him
So deft and quick by foaming edge
Of tide; running with fairy-like grace,
By shining pebbles on sea-soaked sand.
Picking morsels bereft of waves,
          One could only admire.

Who needs Roses?

What ambition! To garnish the winter;
    To crack ice; to emulate snow;
Thrust heavenward such fine elfin texture
    When little or nothing will grow.
And imagine! The core of the matter
    Where teardrop in teardrop so form
That defying all hazards of weather
    Come Candlemass, snowdrops adorn.

Stalwart

So swiftly to the highest perch
At first of rainfalls droplets –
A herald of the darkling skies
His foraging forgotten.

Why flute and trill on lifeless branch
Wind-tossed but quite unruffled,
While lightnings flash and thunders roll?
It really has me puzzled.

Maybe he's laying claim to worms
Or juicy snails for later
But surely this could wait awhile
Until the storm's abated.

Regardless then his notes ring out
Above the gale and clamour.
It seems he's made the storm his stage;
The lightning for his glamour.

But there his presence comforts me
Etched stark on slatey heavens.
So sing Storm-cock until a sigh
Will barely stir your feathers.

(In memory of Tom … returned to
the wild against all the odds.)

The Heritage Trail

We met a man at Skinningrove:
"Nice day fo't time o' year"
"We're staying down at Staithes," we said.
He said, "You mean at Staithes.
If Captain Cook apprenticed was
At Staithes but spelt it Staithes
I'm not surprised he took to ships
And voyaged o'er the waves."

Note: Staithes is pronounced Steers by all the local people.

What's that Grebe?

Just a bird.
An elegant bird on calm waters gliding:
Swiftly and silently diving,
Swimming with as much grace below as above
To feed on small fish and aquatic life.
But privileged to watch the Spring display:
"Oh – *mating*", I hear you say.
(they could quite as easily mate without')
Only God – in his infinite wisdom –
Would apportion such heights of ecstasy to
Just a bird.

Tree of Life

Here in the midst of the garden of peacefulness
Grows a magical 'faraway' tree.
Its beginning harks back to another in Eden
Where were apples that so tempted Eve.
Now in moments of thinking and mindfulness
My eyes wander skywards to see
High up in those branches so ancient yet strong
Rosebuds clamber, cascade to be free.

A whisper weaves into the silence.
"I am the vine, you are the branches."

Lord, in our quest for the perfect enlightenment
Vine and Tree seem to merge into one.
We climb or we scramble, like Rose we would ramble:
When at last with our efforts all done
We've left far behind our worldly environment,
Our vision – a crown to be won.
Like cascades of roses we blossom anew and
Burst with the angels into fine song.

Pleshey, May 2018

Drops of Life

The Cherry Fairies came and cried
And dropped their tears of healing balm
Among the fallen trees.
How else through droughts did they survive?
Thus thriving untold arms reached high
And sought the kiss of heaven.

The Cherry Fairies came last night
With petalled skirt and dewy wings,
Their tears were tears of joy!
The barren valley white delight.
In one unbroken rapid, surged
A cherry-blossom river.

Scrubs Wood, 1992

Down among the Dead Men!

When all is darkness:
Soundless eeriness:
Then spectres dance
In silent ring-o-roses
By the graveyard.

With dawn and light'ning;
Sunshine's brightening,
The scene has changed:
Only the gooseb'ries know the
Name of the game.

Manse fruit garden,
covered with net curtains.

UNSPOKEN

Softly we wake to a summer snow:
On every palm-leaved tree
A thousand wax-white candles glow;
Each hedgerow dripping hawthorn boughs
On 'parsley's surfy sea.

Surely we dream of an autumn's fire:
Haws raging, blazing red.
Entangling 'parsley's starry spire:
With chestnut brown and amber pools
Beguiling where they're shed.

Return

If I were to live to greater maturity
I'd look back with wonder at days gone by,
Memories aglow as a star-spangled sky;
And enticing my soul to velvet eternity,
The momentry magic of one nightingale,
Enchantment's supreme serenade.

Advent Hope

We walked to church, the country route,
As most folk did in days gone by;
December breathing icy mist
Cloaked hedge and all in feathered white.
Oak leaves were Frosties underfoot;
Holly's rime curvaceous clinging;
Old orchard trees as choir-boys stood
Thrummed loud with fieldfares' caroling.
We hardly saw, the mist still swirled,
But Jack had seen. Who was this leant
So drunkenly against the hedge –
No crows to scare redundant friend?
He held out snowy garlands.
And from the rose leaves edged with death,
Stems thick with nature's armaments
I saw a ghostly image rise;
The perfect, glowing Flower of Peace.

Why can't we see you, Child in the manger,
    Simply but special, as those shepherds did?
Why bury you deeply in mountains of presents
    With twizzles of tinsel a crown for your head?
And is that you crying? We too are despairing,
    For two thousand years of warring and strife
Has taught us so little. The world seems to spin
    In the carnage of knowledge: the wastage of life.

How do you view us, mantled in anger,
    Spending our time in a flurry of jobs?
Should we but listen we'd hear, not the angels,
    But the every-day pain of the every-day mobs.
Oh help us this Season, by strength of your spirit
    To curb our resentment of wrongs in the past.
To look with clear vision, as *you* did in your lifetime,
    And hold out *our* hands in a peace that will last.

SERVIETTE

"Watch this Gran," young Jasmine said,
"You fold the paper, so …
Just here … and here … and here.
Then flip, repeat those folds again."
So swiftly were the angles made
Each crease and paper turn
I soon was lost, my mind agog –
What purpose had this 'game'?

Origami as an art
Reminds us all of love:
We're building up: a fold,
A turn – geometry IS life.
When hearts are caught as magic wrought:
(Those fingers deft revealed
A perfect paper rose – outclassed!)
Here blooms a caring wife.

Winter Warmer

Valentine is here again
    Arrows at the quiver.
With snow and ice to spoil his aim
    And bodies all a-shiver,
He may well find his arrows dart
    More painful places that the heart!

September Moon

There's a huge moon tonight
Like a new-mint coin.
Polished and bright.
Each garden, each hedgerow
The fields and the woods
All are aglow
As fall silvery moonbeams,
And the tawny cries,
Leaving his dreams
To perch in the oak tree's
Stark black form, seeing
But quite unseen.
Beyond this the ground mist
Rises and shimmers
As snow sun-kissed;
With bodiless treetops
Like islands floating
Among the floss;
While the owl afar
Replies to her love
'Neath dwindling stars.
They'll be hunting quite soon
For mice ashine in
September moon.

The Bluebell Line

A thread of silver winds its way
Between the treeclad hills.
The station stands alone and sad,
No more the noisy thrills.
The hissing, huffing, the puffing
Steam and the whistles blown.
No rush to board the waiting train,
Clip-cloop of tickets shown.
Nought but the whispering ghosts who meet
To gossip on the stair,
The cool stone stair of the subway.
No feet now scurry there.

What of these people here today
Who wait with eager eyes
And ears so pricked for the whistle
The little engine cries.
"Here she comes!" the shout goes out,
Echoes across the line.
Excitement flies, for everyone
The days of steam do pine.
They wish once more a train to board,
A train that puffs out smoke,
One that chugs and chuffs and toots:
They all love trains these folk.

The engine comes. She's spick and span;
Polished up like new,
Her coaches clean and tidy, though
There are of course but few.
The whistle shrieks and off we go,
Our trip to Sheffield Park
While up above can still be heard
A sweetly singing lark.
We pass the fields quite gold with corn;
The wood where in the spring
Bluebells grow, but where just now a
Lonesome blackbird sings.

Our heads hang from the windows
So's not to miss the fun
Of seeing the station loom ahead
At the end of the run.
We sniff the smoke that Fenchurch makes,
It's such a lovely smell.
Why some prefer a diesel train
Is very hard to tell.
Oh dear, oh dear, she's slowing down,
And there, along the track,
Is Sheffield Park. But nevermind
We've still the journey back.

THE GOLDEN TOUCH

With a whisper of chill as the dawn breaks,
Eyed vaguely by one sleepy star,
Autumn comes dancing on tiptoe
Through soft-spangled dew-laden grass.
She stretched her hands to the hedgerow
Where Bellbine determined and bold
Struggled, scrambled, high up trees rambled:
Now trails only hearts of pure gold.
Some neat pirouettes under the willows,
And there in the ardour of morn
Leaves gleam, as billowy tresses
Fresh-washed on the gentle breeze borne.
She lifts high her skirts for the woodland
Where showers of gilded leaves sigh,
Creating for Her a rich carpet
While Time says the dawning must fly.
Amid twirling leaves on She still dances,
Gold fungi at once strew Her way,
Then touching Her toes to pay homage –
She's gone – leaving sunbeams at play.

The Last Rose

It was a difficult year for the roses:
Spring drought; intense heat; and siroccos.
Despite this they managed to blossom
Surprising us all with perfections of form,
Scenting our wanderings – lifting our morns.
But somehow the last one was special.
Survival had smoothed every petal;
Curvacious in greeting a secretive dawn
Resigned to brief beauty as springtime reborn.

God also said:
I give you all plants. Genesis 1 v. 29

Did God create a rose –
    Symbol of human love?
Who formed these petals?
- Such silken gold befits the robe of kings.
Whose fragrance drenched the very heart
    Exclusively to bring
The nectar seekers, bees and bumbles
    Hunting far and wide.
Who shaped it so, this perfect rose
    The choice of many a bride?
    Man played a part –
    But God it was
    Whose vision we can't know
    Who gave *to* us *all* plants.
May God, whose passion stirred the rose
    Live on in you and me.

ROYAL BIRTH DAY

While Chapel meadow grasses grew
Some deep-down secrets chewed and chewed
Until beneath a misty moon
The larvae climbed and spun cocoons
Of gold, on stems toward the sky.

While Kate gives birth to little George
Our Six-spot Burnet Moths emerge
Wing to a Knapweed, feed and rest.
Resplendent in their regal vests
They glad the heart, delight the eye.

…

Printed in Great Britain
by Amazon

64364372R00054